THE BATTLE AGAINST
BOREDOM

How to Draw Cartoons

THE HORNED AVENGER™

Ray Nelson • Ben Adams • Douglas Kelly

A Division of Thomas Nelson Publishers
Since 1798

For other life-changing resources, visit us at
www.thomasnelson.com

THE HORNED AVENGER

Story:
Ray Nelson

Pencils & Inking:
Ben Adams
Ray Nelson
Douglas Kelly

Animal Trainer:
Mike McLane

Costumes:
Chris Nelson
Holly McLane

Computer:
Ben Adams
Matt Adams
Marcus Gannuscio
Brud Giles
Julie Hansen
Kyle Holveck
Ray Nelson
Aaron Peeples
Kari Rasmussen

SOMETIME IN
THE FUTURE ...

Published in Nashville, Tennessee, by Tommy Nelson®, a Division of Thomas Nelson, Inc.

Scripture quoted from the *International Children's Bible®*, *New Century Version®*, © 1986, 1988, 1999 by Tommy Nelson®, a Division of Thomas Nelson, Inc., Nashville, TN 37214. Used by permission.

Tommy Nelson® books may be purchased in bulk for educational, business, fundraising, or sales promotional use. For information, please e-mail SpecialMarkets@ThomasNelson.com.

ISBN: 1-4003-0662-0

Printed in the United States of America

05 06 07 08 PHX 5 4 3 2 1

OUT OF THE RUBBLE CLIMBS THE HORNED AVENGER, THE ONLY HOPE FOR PLANET SPERANZA. A HULKING FIGURE, HE PULLS HIMSELF TO THE TOP OF THE WRECKAGE TO SURVEY THE SCENE BELOW. HIS MUSCLES RIPPLE AS HE SWINGS HIS MAMMOTH HEAD FROM LEFT TO RIGHT. WHAT WAS ONCE A LAUGHING PLANET IS NOW THE PLAYGROUND OF BOREDOM . . . BARON VON BOREDOM!!!!
HEY, MUSCLE BOY! DO YOU THINK YOU COULD QUIT FLEXING FOR JUST A SECOND AND HELP ME UP?
OH, SORRY, BLT.
AN UNLIKELY PAIR INDEED, THE HORNED AVENGER AND BLT PREPARE TO FULFILL THEIR DESTINY. THE HORNED AVENGER'S FAITH IN THE CREATOR HAS GIVEN HIM THE ABILITY TO MOVE MOUNTAINS. "IF YOUR FAITH IS AS BIG AS A MUSTARD SEED, YOU CAN SAY THIS TO THE MOUNTAIN, 'MOVE FROM HERE TO THERE.' AND THE MOUNTAIN WILL MOVE. ALL THINGS WILL BE POSSIBLE FOR YOU." (MATTHEW 17:20)

DO YOU REMEMBER, BLT, WHEN SPERANZA WAS A PLANET FILLED WITH LAUGHTER? WHEN BRIGHT COLORS FILLED THE SKY AND CREATIVITY COULD BE FOUND JUST AROUND THE CORNER?

WHEN THE GREAT CREATOR SPOKE EVERYTHING INTO BEING, HE GAVE US ALL A TREMENDOUS GIFT. EVERY CHILD IS BORN WITH INCREDIBLE CREATIVE POWER THAT COMES FROM THE CREATOR. IF THAT CREATIVITY IS NURTURED, THE CHILDREN WILL HAVE THE ABILITY TO REALIZE THAT WE WERE ALL CREATED TO KNOW HIM.

IT WAS AS IF THE PLANET HAD BEEN FOREVER COVERED IN DARKNESS. IT HAD, IN REALITY, ONLY BEEN A FEW SHORT MONTHS. HOW COULD THIS TERRIBLE CATASTROPHE HAVE HAPPENED?

HOW COULD THIS TERRIBLE CATASTROPHE HAVE HAPPENED?

4

IT ALL BEGAN . . . WHEN A SMALL BOY NAMED ELMER WAINWRIGHT
TURNED IN AN ART PROJECT. ELMER WAS QUITE PROUD OF THIS PROJECT.
HE HAD DRAWN A DETAILED SCENE OF ALIEN SPACE MONSTERS EATING THE
HEADS OFF A CROWD OF FRIGHTENED TOWNSPEOPLE. (ELMER'S DRAWING
WAS KIND OF GROSS, BUT IT WAS A REALLY CREATIVE PIECE OF WORK.)
WHEN ELMER TURNED IN HIS MASTERPIECE, HE RECEIVED A HARSH LECTURE
FROM HIS TEACHER. HE WAS TOLD THAT GRASS IS ALWAYS GREEN AND
SKIES ARE ALWAYS BLUE. THE TEACHER ALSO SAID THAT ALIENS EATING
TOWNSPEOPLE WASN'T AN APPROPRIATE TOPIC FOR ART AND THAT WE
SHOULD ALWAYS COLOR INSIDE THE LINES.

THIS CRUSHED POOR ELMER. EVERY OUNCE
OF CREATIVITY WAS SUCKED FROM THE
LITTLE BOY. THEN ONE DAY, AFTER WATCHING
A TWELVE-HOUR "BRADY BUNCH" MARATHON,
LITTLE ELMER WAINWRIGHT STOOD UP
AND YELLED . . .

I'M NOT GOING
TO TAKE IT
ANYMOOORE!

"FROM THIS DAY FORWARD, I WILL BE KNOWN AS
BARON VON BOREDOM AND THE REST OF THE WORLD WILL
SUFFER ALONG WITH ME. IF I CANNOT BE CREATIVE, I WILL
DRAG EVERY OTHER LIVING CREATURE INTO THE DEPTHS OF
BOREDOM WITH ME. THIS PLANET WILL NEVER AGAIN SEE
GRASS THAT IS GREEN OR SKIES THAT ARE BLUE!"

5

AND SO, MY LITTLE PILE OF PORK RINDS, THAT IS HOW BARON VON BOREDOM CAME TO BE. THIS DISMAL PLACE IN WHICH WE LIVE IS ALL THE WORK OF BOREDOM . . . BARON VON BOREDOM.
DON'T LOOK NOW, H.A., BUT SOME OF BOREDOM'S WORK IS HEADING THIS WAY AND THEY DON' LOOK TOO FRIENDLY!

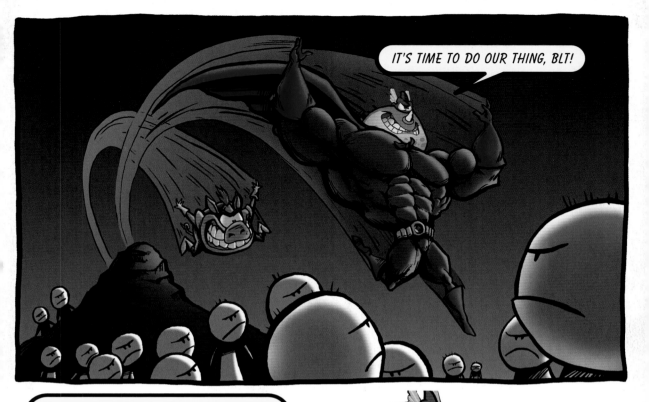

CARTOONING IS ALL ABOUT TAKING CHANCES AND TRYING NEW STUFF. DON'T WORRY ABOUT MAKING EVERY DRAWING PERFECT. DON'T SPEND MOST OF YOUR TIME ERASING. IF YOU THINK YOU'VE MESSED UP, KEEP GOING. YOU NEVER KNOW, YOU MIGHT END UP WITH THE BEST DRAWING YOU'VE EVER DONE.

ALL RIGHT, H.A.! I GET IT! WHERE DO I START?

TOOLS

The first step is to pick the tools that you want to use. All you need is something to draw with and something to draw on. Don't be afraid to experiment with new and unusual tools.

Sketchpad

The sketchpad is one of the most important tools you will work with. You can purchase a sketchpad at any art or variety store. They can cost as little as $2 or as much as $30. If you can't get to the store or don't have any money, gather some old scrap paper and staple it together. Do all of your experimenting and rough drawings in the sketchpad. It's like a storage space for your ideas.

Pens

There are many different styles of pens. Use your sketchbook to try them all. When you test a pen in your sketchbook, write down what kind it is next to the drawing. That way, if you like the style you can use it again. Even simple ballpoint pens can make a great cartoon. Remember: the same pen on different types of paper may look completely different.

Pencils

Pencils come in different shapes, colors, and sizes. Experiment. Try using pencils that are sharp and pencils that are dull. Try using the point and then the side of the lead.

Brushes

If you use ink or paint, you'll need some brushes. Brushes can be very fine for detail work or very thick for coloring large spaces. Always clean your brushes when you're done so they don't get ruined!

Crayons

The Horned Avenger always carries a bunch of crayons. (It doesn't matter how old you are, crayons are great for cartooning.) Crayons allow you to add a quick burst of color to your cartoons. For a great effect, try coloring with crayons and then painting over your cartoon with watercolor paints.

Chalk

Colored chalk can give you some really cool effects. Try chalk on rough paper, a chalkboard, or on the sidewalks around your home.

Paints

Like the other tools, paints come in all different colors and types. Watercolors and acrylics are great to use because of their bright colors. They are also easier to clean up than oil paints.

Photocopier

A photocopier is a gold mine for a cartoonist. Your teacher or parents might be able to make copies for you. There are also stores that specialize in making copies. Take one of your really awesome cartoons and make a bunch of copies. This will allow you to experiment with different colors. Another neat trick is to slowly pull the cartoon as it is being copied. This will distort your drawing, giving you some strange results. All of this is fun and doesn't ruin the original drawing.

Cardboard

Try drawing your cartoons on cardboard. You can cut them out, and they will stand up by themselves.

STONE AGE CAVE PEOPLE USED TO DRAW ON CAVE WALLS WITH BARK AND BERRIES.

Paper

You might not know it, but there are thousands of types of paper. Some paper is smooth and some is bumpy. Some paper is waterproof and some really soaks up paint and ink. Try different types of paper with various pens, paints, and pencils.

Napkins

At some time or another, you'll have to wait for your food in the cafeteria or a restaurant. Next time this happens, grab a bunch of napkins and start drawing. Ballpoint pen ink on a napkin looks great.

Old Magazines

Grab a bunch of old magazines. Then pretend you're Dr. Frankenstein and cut out body parts. Glue the different body parts together to create wacky new cartoon characters.

Old Yearbooks

Ask parents or friends to dig up all of their old yearbooks. Yearbooks are the best places to find really weird names for your characters. You'll also get good ideas for cartoon faces and hairstyles.

Mixing Stuff

Try mixing all of your cartooning tools. Paint a background and glue a magazine monster character to it. Try drawing crayon characters and painting a watercolor background over it.

Modeling Clay

Clay offers a whole different world for cartooning. Take clay and build characters that you have drawn. Sometimes it is more difficult to build a character out of clay than it is to draw one because you have to decide what the character looks like from the side, back, and front!

LET'S GET STARTED, SHALL WE?

LET'S GIVE HIM THE STANDARD HUMAN FACE, H.A.!

BLT! HAVE YOU FORGOTTEN THE ONLY RULE TO CARTOONING? THE ONLY RULE TO CARTOONING IS . . .

THERE ARE NO RULES!

NO MATTER HOW HARD YOU TRY, YOU CAN'T DRAW A CARTOON WRONG. IF YOU WANTED TO GIVE THIS STICK FIGURE TWENTY-SEVEN EYEBALLS AND GREEN HAIR, YOU COULD. IF YOU WANTED TO GIVE HIM A COW'S HEAD AND THE BODY OF A HAMSTER, YOU COULD.

THERE ARE NO RULES

WHEN YOU ARE CARTOONING! DON'T WORRY ABOUT MESSING UP. SOME OF MY BEST CARTOONS WERE DRAWINGS THAT I THOUGHT I HAD MESSED UP. INSTEAD OF STARTING OVER, I KEPT DRAWING AND ENDED UP WITH SOMETHING NEW, COOL, AND UNEXPECTED!

LET'S START BY GIVING THIS POOR GUY A SET OF EYES. THE EYES ARE THE MOST EXPRESSIVE PART OF A CARTOON CHARACTER. YOUR CARTOONS SHOULD HAVE STRONG PERSONALITIES AND EMOTIONS. EYES WILL HELP GIVE YOUR CHARACTERS STRONG PERSONALITIES.

EYES

pupils

dots · circles · teardrops · baggy eyes · droopy eyelids

big bucks · crazy eyes

YOU KNOW WHAT I LIKE TO DO? I LIKE TO MAKE THE PUPILS DIFFERENT SHAPES. I DRAW DOLLAR SIGNS WHEN A CHARACTER HAS FOUND LOTS OF MONEY. I DRAW THE PUPILS IN THE SHAPE OF LITTLE HEARTS WHEN THE CHARACTER IS IN LOVE. SOMETIMES I JUST MOVE THE PUPILS AROUND OR MAKE THEM DIFFERENT SIZES.

evil eyes · cute eyes

worried · angry · surprised

accusing · blank stare · tired

11

NOSES

The nose is the easiest feature to draw on a face. Start with a basic shape, such as a circle or a triangle. Don't be afraid to adjust the size and proportion of the nose shape.

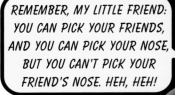

REMEMBER, MY LITTLE FRIEND: YOU CAN PICK YOUR FRIENDS, AND YOU CAN PICK YOUR NOSE, BUT YOU CAN'T PICK YOUR FRIEND'S NOSE. HEH, HEH!

Use a circle for a nose.

Draw a C for a nose.

Try a clover-leaf shape.

Use two sides of a triangle for a pointed nose.

Try stretching the nose down.

See how big you can make the nose.

Try turning the nose up and coloring in the nostril.

A bumpy pickle makes a weird nose. Add warts and hair for extra fun!

You can also add nostrils to a nose.

SNIFF!

SNIFF!

SNIFF!

When using shapes, such as a circle or a C, don't get stuck using only one version of that shape. Try stretching or squashing the shape for different looks.

normal   stretched   big

squashed   small

MOUTHS

One of the best ways to make a cartoon mouth is to draw a line. Try different types of lines—long, short, straight, crooked, squiggled, and jagged. After you get good at making line mouths, try a few open mouths. Don't forget to draw the teeth and tongue.

Here's a simple-line mouth.

Raise the line under the nose.

Use a jagged line.

Make a short-line mouth.

Use a slanted-line mouth.

Wrap the mouth all the way around the nose.

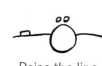

Try squiggling the line.

Try using a triangle, then add a tongue.

Try squishing the triangle.

Add a tongue and some teeth to an open mouth.

Not all teeth are perfect. Try different sizes and shapes.

Droop a tongue from the line. Add some slobber.

Draw a mouth from the side.

13

Horned Avenger Hint

What characters say or think tells us a lot about their personalities. Are they mean or nice? Serious or funny? Are they self-confident or do they get jealous easily? Dialogue can show us important clues about the plot or get the reader to laugh at a funny joke. When you draw your characters, what types of things are they going to say or think?

BODY SHAPES

When you first build cartoon characters, use simple shapes for their bodies.

circles and ovals

triangles

squares and rectangles

stretch shapes

MALE

Different body shapes and sizes create different personalities. Remember to exaggerate!

A muscleman has a wide chest.

Experiment with arm and leg length.

Expand the tummy for a cartoon couch potato.

Kids have big heads and little bodies.

A basketball player has a stretched-out body.

FEMALE

Cartoon women look different than male cartoons. Exaggerate different features to create even more characters.

Use a triangle for a little girl's dress.

Try a bigger, rounder figure.

Horned Avenger Hint
Try moving a character's belt line for a new look.

Exaggerate the pinched waist to create a cartoon supermodel.

HEAD SHAPES

HOLY CARTOON CRANIUM, BLT, THIS IS TOUGH!

YOU SAID IT, BIG BOY! I'M GETTIN' A HEADACHE!

The head shape for a cartoon character doesn't always have to be round like a real human head. Think of a cartoon head as a big water balloon. When you squish the top, the bottom gets bigger. When you squeeze the bottom, the top gets bigger. Any shape can make a great cartoon head. In pencil, lightly sketch the shape you are going to use. You can then use the shape as a guide to build the head.

circle

square

oval stretched tall

triangle pointing up

triangle pointing down

oval squished flat

Horned Avenger Hint
Ears can be made with a C shape and a backward C shape. Ears can be placed up high on a head or really low on a head. Try all kinds of different locations for the ears.

COMPOUND HEAD SHAPES

A compound shape is two shapes put together. Mix different head shapes to create a new cartoon character.

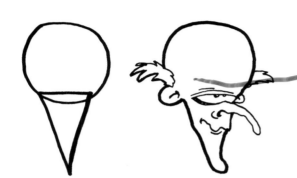

Place a circle on top of a triangle for an ice cream cone shape.

Add a rectangle to the top of a circle.

Try a triangle on top of a square.

Have the upper lip stick out for an overbite.

Have the lower lip stick out for an underbite.

PLACING FEATURES

Try creating different faces with the same head shape. Draw several circles the same size, and then move the features around the face. Also, experiment with different-sized features for a new look.

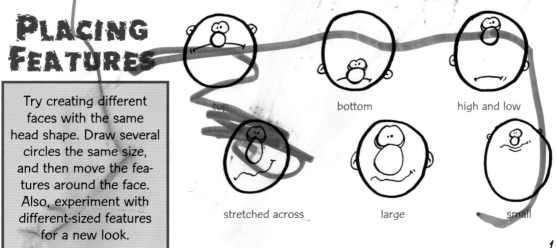

top

bottom

high and low

stretched across

large

small

17

To make a character successful, you need to add details. One of the best details you can add to a character is hair. Using a different hairstyle changes not only the look of a character, but also its personality. Be inventive with the hairstyles you use. For reference, look through old magazines or yearbooks for different hairstyles.

MARCIA, MARCIA, MARCIA

MILITARY

Horned Avenger Hint

Mix and match the hair that you add to your characters. Don't forget that hair grows in places other than on the tops of heads. Try different styles of hair, such as mustaches, beards, sideburns, eyebrows, and even nose and leg hair.

PUNK PORKER

SANTA PORK

THE KING

DOLLY PORKER

ROCKER

MALL HAIR

MAD SCIENTIST

HAIR CLUB FOR PIGS

HANDLEBAR PIG 19

EXPRESSIONS

YOU ARE ONE GOOD-LOOKIN' HERO!

The best way to learn how to draw expressions is to look in a mirror. Study what every part of your face does when you make an expression. Look at your features and then try to draw that expression in your sketchpad. With practice, you'll be able to draw all kinds of expressions without even thinking about it.

GRRRRRR!

HAPPY, HAPPY, JOY, JOY!

YOU GOTTA BE KIDDIN' ME!

IT FIGURES!

CHEEEESE!

BOO-BOO LIP

HUBBA, HUBBA!

THIS CAN'T BE HAPPENING!

BRAIN CRAMP

20

OUCH! OUCH! OOOOO!

WORRIED

NOT IMPRESSED

HEH HEH HEH!

AUGHHH!

WHAT ARE YOU LOOKIN' AT?!

WAHHHHH!

OOOOOPS!

ZZZZZZZ

BONK!

DID I DO THAT?

Horned Avenger Hint

Don't underestimate the importance of giving your characters extreme expressions. People love characters with personality. Expressions help give your characters personality.

EXTREME EXPRESSIONS

WHEN DRAWING YOUR CHARACTERS, DON'T BE AFRAID TO MAKE THEIR EXPRESSIONS **REALLY** WILD. PEOPLE LOVE IT WHEN EYES BUG OUT AND JAWS DROP TO THE GROUND.

EXPLODING EYES

WOW

HYPNOTIZED

JAW DROP

VOLCANO EARS

LOVESTRUCK

PUTTING IT TOGETHER

Putting a character together starts with many rough sketches. Mix and match the simple head and body shapes you've learned so far until you get something you like. Then combine different facial features for new looks. The possibilities are endless, so don't stop with your first try.

1. Start your character by roughing in simple head and body shapes. Add some rough arms and legs.

2. Try different facial features.

3. Add details, such as hair and clothing. Try coloring in your character with crayons, markers, or paints.

PLACING HEADS

Try moving the head to different locations on the body.

way down on the chest

on top of the body

at the end of a long neck

24

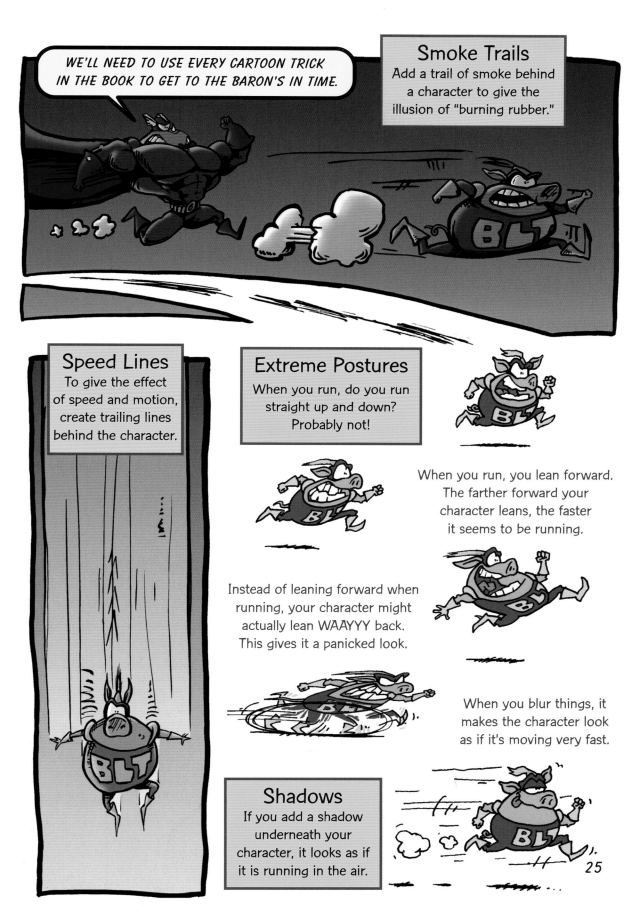

WE'LL NEED TO USE EVERY CARTOON TRICK IN THE BOOK TO GET TO THE BARON'S IN TIME.

Smoke Trails
Add a trail of smoke behind a character to give the illusion of "burning rubber."

Speed Lines
To give the effect of speed and motion, create trailing lines behind the character.

Extreme Postures
When you run, do you run straight up and down? Probably not!

When you run, you lean forward. The farther forward your character leans, the faster it seems to be running.

Instead of leaning forward when running, your character might actually lean WAAYYY back. This gives it a panicked look.

When you blur things, it makes the character look as if it's moving very fast.

Shadows
If you add a shadow underneath your character, it looks as if it is running in the air.

26

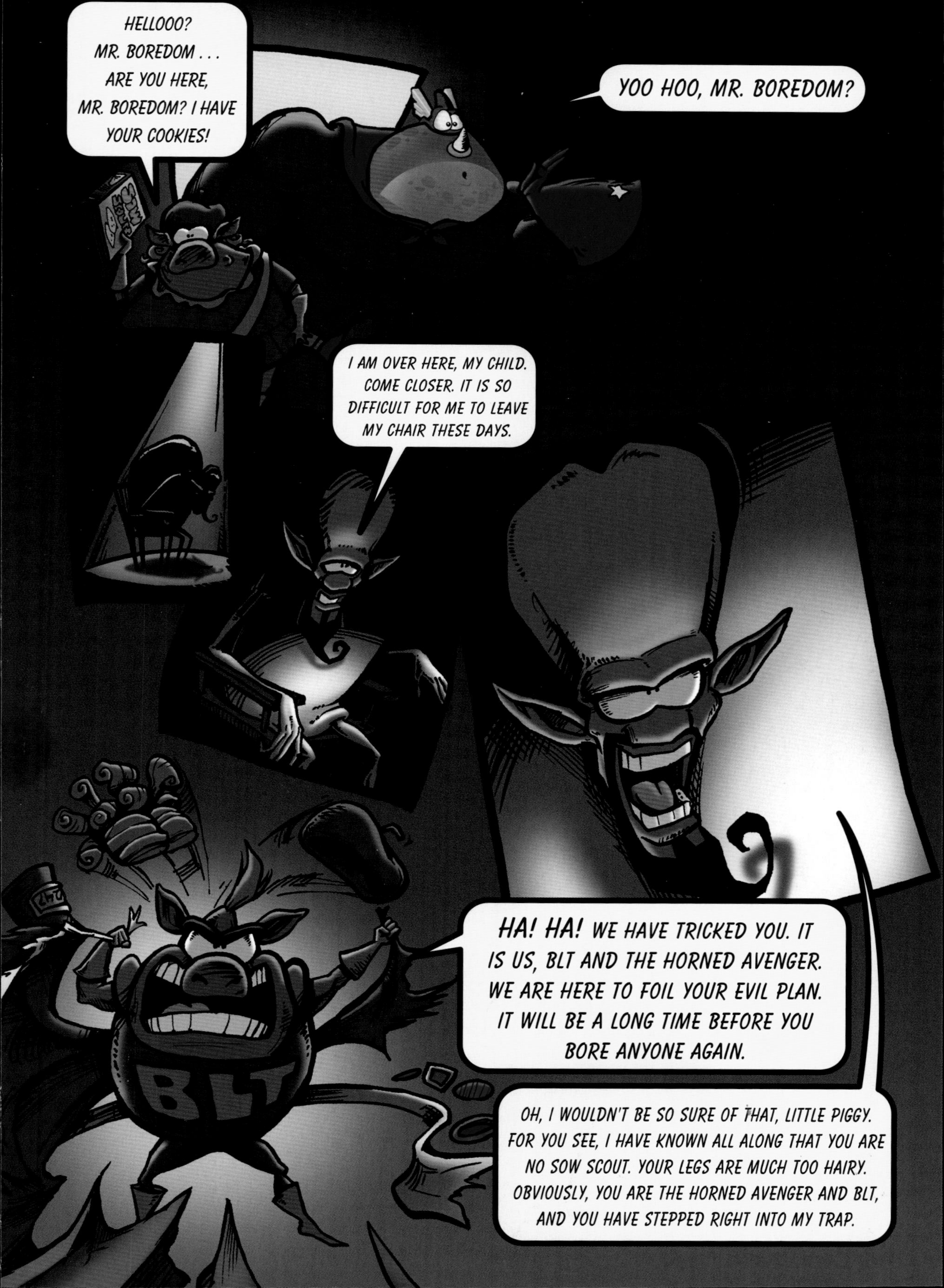
HELLOOO? MR. BOREDOM . . . ARE YOU HERE, MR. BOREDOM? I HAVE YOUR COOKIES!
YOO HOO, MR. BOREDOM?
I AM OVER HERE, MY CHILD. COME CLOSER. IT IS SO DIFFICULT FOR ME TO LEAVE MY CHAIR THESE DAYS.
HA! HA! WE HAVE TRICKED YOU. IT IS US, BLT AND THE HORNED AVENGER. WE ARE HERE TO FOIL YOUR EVIL PLAN. IT WILL BE A LONG TIME BEFORE YOU BORE ANYONE AGAIN.
OH, I WOULDN'T BE SO SURE OF THAT, LITTLE PIGGY. FOR YOU SEE, I HAVE KNOWN ALL ALONG THAT YOU ARE NO SOW SCOUT. YOUR LEGS ARE MUCH TOO HAIRY. OBVIOUSLY, YOU ARE THE HORNED AVENGER AND BLT, AND YOU HAVE STEPPED RIGHT INTO MY TRAP.
BLT

30

OUR HEROES FINALLY AWAKE AFTER A CRUEL, BRUTAL, AND PAINFULLY BORING 17-HOUR VIEWING OF THE VON BOREDOM VACATION SLIDES. THEY FIND THEMSELVES TIED TO A PLANK BY REALLY STRONG ROPE, TRAVELING AT A HIGH RATE OF SPEED TOWARD AN UNUSUALLY LARGE AND VERY SHARP SAW BLADE. THE FUTURE OF THESE TWO BRAVE BUT SIMPLE DOERS OF GOOD SEEMS BLEAK AT BEST!

HANDS

Speaking of grabbing, some of the most difficult things to draw are hands. Don't get discouraged! If you practice drawing hands, you will get better. At first, don't try to draw all of the joints and details of the hand. Use a circle for the palm and simple, rounded fingers.

1. Draw a circle at the end of the arm.

2. Add a thumb sticking out one side.

3. Add three or four fingers.

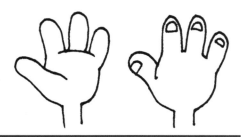

Draw long and thin fingers.

For a baby, try short and stubby hands.

When drawing the palm side, extend the thumb across the palm. If you're drawing the back of a hand, add fingernails.

MORE HANDS

34

WHEN WE LEFT THE HORNED AVENGER AND HIS SALTY SIDEKICK, BLT, THEY HAD CHASED THE EVIL BARON VON BOREDOM INTO THE CITY ZOO. TIME IS RUNNING OUT FOR OUR HEROES TO CAPTURE VON BOREDOM AND RETURN EARTH TO ITS EXCITING AND COLORFUL WAYS.
MY SENSES ARE TINGLING AGAIN, LITTLE BUDDY. . . . VON BOREDOM MUST BE NEAR!
YEAH, YEAH . . . JUST A MINUTE. MY TIGHTS ARE RIDING UP ON ME.

LOT-O-PAPER
PROPERTY OF H.A.
WE MUST FOCUS, BLT! WE MUST LISTEN TO THE CREATOR'S LEADING.
TO CAPTURE VON BOREDOM, WE MUST THINK LIKE CRIMINALS. WE MUST DIG DOWN DEEP AND . . . BLT, WHERE ARE YOU GOING?
WOOOSH
HUH?
WE CAN'T GO HUNTIN' FOR BAD GUYS ON AN EMPTY STOMACH, NOW CAN WE, H.A.! I GOT A TURBO TUB O' ZOO CORN WITH EXTRA GREASE.
YOU DIDN'T WANT ANYTHING, DID YA, HORN BOY?
ZOO CORN
A PIG'S SERVING FOR THE HOG IN YOU!!

> *I WILL CALL ON THE CREATOR FOR SUPER POWERS OF FAITH TO HELP TURN THIS POOR CREATURE BACK INTO A PROUD MEMBER OF THE ANIMAL KINGDOM.*

GETTING STARTED

Here are some basic steps that the Horned Avenger and BLT suggest to get started cartooning:

1. **Get Comfortable.** Make sure that you have the necessary space, materials, and lighting for drawing cartoons.

2. **Research.** Before you start drawing, it is very important that you do some research. Go to the library or get on the Internet and study pictures of the animals you want to draw.

3. **Brainstorm.** Pick up your pencil and make a list of the first four or five features that come to mind when you think of your animal. For example, if you are drawing an elephant, the four most memorable features might be a trunk, tusks, big floppy ears, and a gigantic body.

4. **Exaggerate.** To turn your animal into a cartoon, exaggerate the notable features. If your animal has a long nose, draw a really, really, really long nose.

5. **Do Rough Sketches.** Remember that you are not doing a finished illustration. Spend your early drawing time doing rough sketches. The sketching stage is for experimenting and choosing basic shapes and characteristics. Fill in the details after you do a bunch of rough sketches.

6. **Have Fun!** If you aren't having fun, you need to put your drawing supplies away and relax. Go back to your drawings when you feel rested and are ready to have fun again.

7. **Think!** Isn't it awesome how creative God's creatures are? Challenge yourself to be creative as you design your animals.

PROPERTY OF H.A.

GOBS -O- PENS

Gut Bomb Pop Korn Jubilee

ZEBRAS

Now that you know how to get started cartooning, help the Horned Avenger and BLT transform the boring zebras back into their old striped selves.

1. Start by drawing some cartoon eyes. Add a snout or nose. The snout starts under the eyes, droops down, and then curls back up into a silly grin.

2. Draw a circle around the eyes and mouth. Add nostrils by drawing two dots and putting an upside-down U over them. To make a goofy tongue, add a U to the bottom of the snout.

3. Add two ears by drawing leaf shapes on top of the head.

4. Draw two lines coming down from the head to make a great neck. The neck can be any length. Use a simple circle for the body, then add a tail. Draw legs in the same way you drew the neck

Use the basic body shape of the zebra to create other hoofed animals, such as cows, horses, camels, and giraffes.

5. Draw the stripes and punk-rock mane. Hooves can be made by drawing a triangle with the flat edge at the bottom.

Try having your animal stand on its hind legs like a human.

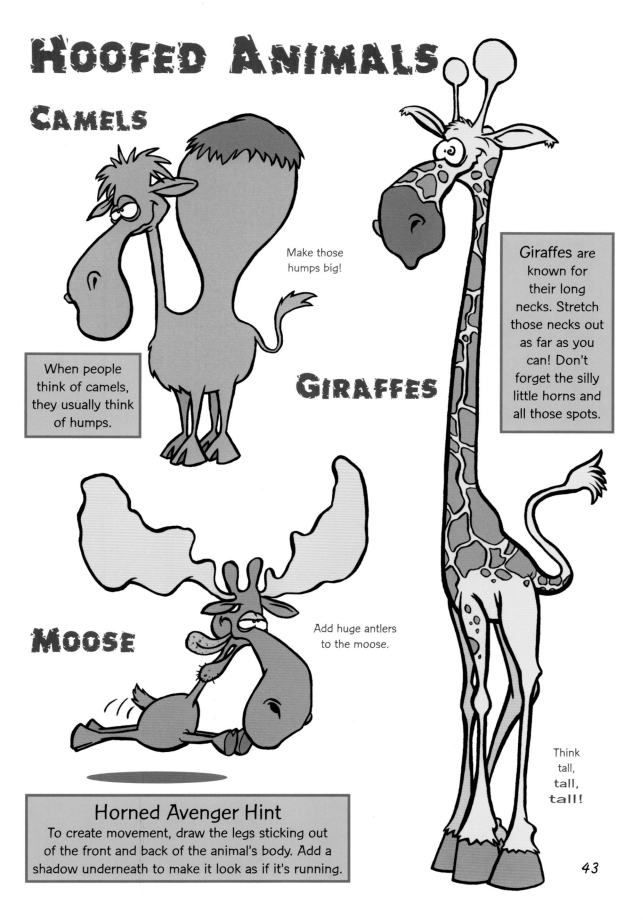

Hoofed Animals

Camels

Make those humps big!

When people think of camels, they usually think of humps.

Giraffes

Giraffes are known for their long necks. Stretch those necks out as far as you can! Don't forget the silly little horns and all those spots.

Moose

Add huge antlers to the moose.

Horned Avenger Hint
To create movement, draw the legs sticking out of the front and back of the animal's body. Add a shadow underneath to make it look as if it's running.

Think tall, tall, tall!

WILL THIS MADNESS NEVER END? VON BOREDOM HAS SOILED YET MORE NOBLE BEASTS!

While passing through the lion cage, von Boredom had changed the mighty kings of the jungle into boring stick figures.

The Horned Avenger and BLT can't save these creatures by themselves! Pick up your pencil and help them draw the lions back to normal.

LIONS
(PANTHERA LEO)

1. When drawing cats, start with the eyes. Any type of cartoon eyes will work.

2. Add a nose to your cat. An upside-down triangle (shaped like a piece of pizza) will work perfectly. Any size is fine.

3. On each side of the nose, add half circles. These pouches are for the whiskers.

upside-down
letter U

letter U

4. Add some cheeks and a mouth. Notice that these pieces are just the letter U added to the nose and pouches.

5. Put some ears on his head. Again, use a *U* shape. Don't forget the whiskers.

Horned Avenger Hint

When you finish with the basic shapes, add details. For example, if you're drawing a lion, add a mane. If you're drawing a tiger, add stripes. You'll know what to add and where to put it if you research your animal.

HIPPOS

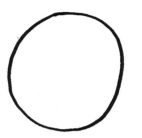

1. Start your hippo by drawing a big circle.

2. Add two smaller circles so that they overlap the big circle.

3. Connect the circles as shown. Add ears, eyes, nostrils, and big goofy teeth. Don't forget the tail.

4. To add legs, just draw little rectangles at the bottom of the big circle. Draw little upside-down *U* shapes for toenails.

If you want to turn your hippo into a rhino, add great big horns on the snout and erase the big, goofy teeth.

AHH, YOU ARE A STUNNING VISION! WAIT FOR ME, MY LITTLE TURTLEDOVE, AND I SHALL RETURN AFTER I DEFEAT THAT NASTY VON BOREDOM!

MONKEYS

oval #1

oval #2

1. Start with a circle.

2. Add eyes and three ovals.

oval #3

3. Add nostrils and lips. The lips should be added at the bottom of the nose oval and the nostrils added at the top.

4. Add rough edges to the oval shapes so they look as if they're covered with hair.

Monkeys have long, thin tails that act almost like extra arms.

Monkeys have long, skinny arms, legs, and bodies.

QUIT MONKEYING AROUND . . . WE NEED TO FIND VON BOREDOM.

Apes

1. Start with an egg shape.

2. For eyes, draw two half circles under a straight line. Add two dots.

forehead wrinkles

nostrils

3. Draw a circle under the egg shape.

punching bag

4. Create an open mouth. Then add a tongue and a little punching bag for the tonsils in the back of the throat. Make each ear with an upside-down letter *U*.

5. Add big, pointy teeth for a fierce-looking ape.

Apes also sport big, broad shoulders and big, round chest muscles.

BIG APE LOVE LITTLE PIG . . . GIVE BIG HUG AND LOTS OF KISSES!

WHAT ARE YOU? BANANAS? WAIT, LET ME REPHRASE THAT!

GATORS

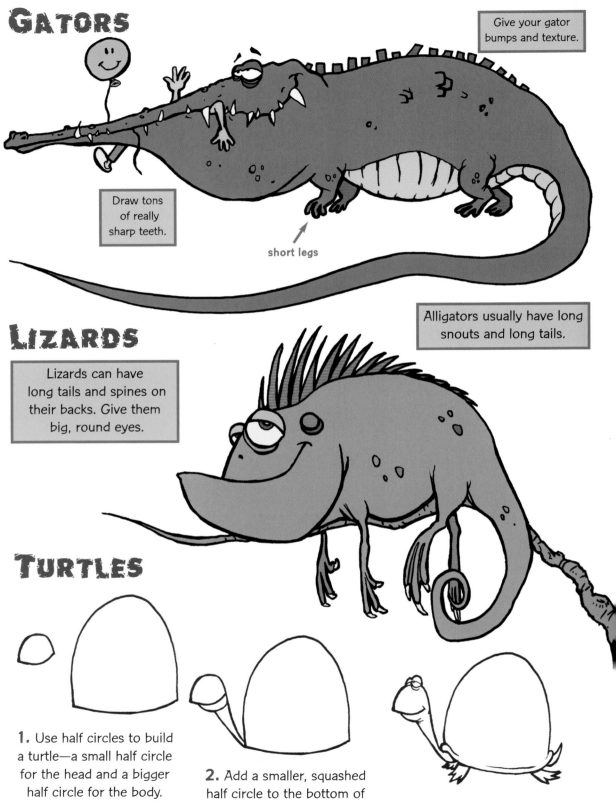

Give your gator bumps and texture.

Draw tons of really sharp teeth.

short legs

Alligators usually have long snouts and long tails.

LIZARDS

Lizards can have long tails and spines on their backs. Give them big, round eyes.

TURTLES

1. Use half circles to build a turtle—a small half circle for the head and a bigger half circle for the body.

2. Add a smaller, squashed half circle to the bottom of the head and two lines down to the body.

3. Add *W* shapes for the feet and some cartoon eyes.

SNAKES

1. Snakes are very easy to draw. Start with a circle and a squiggly line.

2. Copy the shape of the squiggly line, joining the two lines at the tail. Then connect the lines to the circle.

3. Add two eyes on top of the circle. Draw a line across the circle for a mouth.

FROGS

1. To draw frogs, start with two big, round eyes. Add an oval for the body.

2. Draw a line across the oval to make a mouth.

3. Draw some legs. Frogs have long, webbed toes.

THE BARNYARD

SHEEP

Sheep can be drawn like other hoofed animals, but their bodies are a huge wad of wool with a head and four legs. (Start with the basic shapes that you learned on pages 42–43.) Have fun making different-sized sheep—tall, short, fat, and skinny.

"baa baa baa"

PIGS

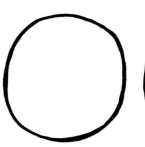  

1. Start with a circle and add another circle for a nose.

2. Add some eyes and a thin line for a mouth.

3. Pigs ears are shaped like leaves. Rectangles work for the legs.

4. You might try adding some human hands and feet and a curly tail.

Pigs are best known for their round snouts, curly tails, and big bellies. Just because a pig is usually round and fat doesn't mean you can't draw a skinny pig. Remember . . . **NO RULES!**

Cows

1. To build a cow, you'll need a snout, eyes, and nostrils.

2. Add some ears and horns. The horns can be any size you wish!

3. Make a neck by drawing two lines from the head. Then draw a fat rectangle to form the body.

4. Give the cow four legs and triangle-shaped hooves.

5. Add a tail and a tongue. Now, your bovine is ready to roll.

Try making your cow run or sit or even dance. The body size and shape may vary quite a bit. Don't be afraid to experiment. Cows can be different colors and patterns. Play around with different color combinations and spot designs.

Don't forget the udder on the cow.

53

Dogs

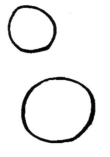

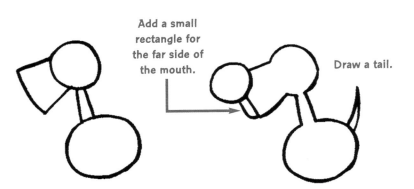

Add a small rectangle for the far side of the mouth.

Draw a tail.

1. Start your dog with two circles.

2. On the top circle, add a rectangle shape extending outward. Connect the circles with two lines for a neck.

3. Add a smaller circle at the end of the rectangle for the nose.

4. Give your dog floppy ears and a tongue. Extend lines down from the body to create the legs.

5. Finish your dog by adding the eyes and feet. Feet are ovals that extend out from the legs. Add several little lines for toes.

For a poodle, try fluffy fur puffs all over your dog's body.

Do some research at the library or on the Internet to find different breeds of dogs to cartoon. Bulldogs have huge bottom jaws. Great Danes have big cheeks. Add a collar for character.

Great Dane

Bulldog

NO RULES!

Horned Avenger Hint
Don't be afraid to get weird with your characters.
Cartoons can do the unexpected. Have a
jack-in-the-box pop out of a kangaroo's
pouch or put a camel in a tuxedo.

RODENTS

Rabbit ears are big, big, big.

When drawing rabbits and rodents—such as mice, squirrels, and beavers—you can use the same face over and over again. For example, a mouse has basically the same face as a rabbit; however, the rabbit will have bigger feet and ears and a fuzzy tail.

RABBITS

A good nose shape is like a slice of pizza.

1. Start with a circle or oval.

2. Add some eyes and a nose.

3. Add an upside-down letter Y to the nose. Then draw two squares for the big, gnawing teeth.

4. Add some big, flat feet and a fluffy cotton tail.

RATS

A rat may have a long or short nose. Don't forget its long tail.

AW, LOOK AT ALL THE CUTE, CUDDLY, FUZZY RODENTS!

THE HORNED AVENGER FEARS NOTHING! WE BELONG TO THE CREATOR. WE HAVE DEFEATED THEM BECAUSE THE CREATOR'S SPIRIT, WHO IS IN US IS GREATER THAN THE EVIL ONE. (1 JOHN 4:4)

DON'T COME ANY CLOSER, HORN BOY! I'M NOT AFRAID TO USE THESE RODENTS! HUNDREDS OF INNOCENT ZOO-GOERS MAY BE HURT!

YOU'RE BLUFFING, VON BOREDOM. EVEN YOU WOULDN'T RISK THE MASS DESTRUCTION CAUSED BY RANDOM RODENT FIRE!

61

NOW, TO ESCAPE THAT GOOFY HERO AND HIS PATHETIC PIG PAL FOR GOOD!

WE'RE CARTOON CHARACTERS. WE SHOULD HAVE SEEN THAT ONE COMING!

YOU'RE RIGHT MY PINK PORTLY PAL. IF WE HAD FOLLOWED ALONG WITH THE THREE MAIN PARTS OF THIS STORY WE WOULD HAVE SEEN THIS COMING.

IT'S SO OBVIOUS NOW. EVERY STORY HAS THREE MAIN PARTS. A BEGINNING, A MIDDLE, AND AN END. EACH PART HAS A SPECIAL JOB. THIS SETBACK IS OBVIOUSLY PART OF THIS STORY'S CLIMAX OR ENDING.

I'M NOT FOLLOWING YOU, H.A.

I JUST MEANT WE SHOULD HAVE SEEN THIS GREAT BIG GIANT MOUNTAIN WE RAN INTO.

TURN THE PAGE, AND YOU'LL SEE WHAT I MEAN.

63

BEGINNING

THE BEGINNING OF ANY GOOD STORY IS WHERE THE READER OR VIEWER LEARNS ALL ABOUT THE SETTING AND CHARACTERS. THE BEGINNING IS ALSO WHERE THE PLOT IS INTRODUCED.

EVERYTHING HAS TO HAPPEN SOMEWHERE. BECAUSE IF SOMETHING HAPPENS NOWHERE, IT'S NOTHING, RIGHT? WAIT...BEFORE OUR BRAINS SEIZE UP, LET'S TRY TO SAY THAT A DIFFERENT WAY. WHEN YOU'RE DEVELOPING A CARTOON STORY, THINK OF DIFFERENT SETTINGS AND THE POSSIBILITIES THEY OFFER.

THINK OF THE AMAZING STORY POSSIBILITIES SUGGESTED BY THESE SETTINGS:
- ▶ A ROCKET LAUNCHING PAD, 90 SECONDS BEFORE LIFTOFF
- ▶ A DOGSLED RACE THROUGH FROZEN ALASKA
- ▶ A LIFEBOAT IN THE MIDDLE OF A STORMY OCEAN

ONCE YOU'VE PICKED A PLACE FOR THINGS TO HAPPEN, YOU NEED SOME CHARACTERS FOR THINGS TO HAPPEN TO. CHARACTERS HELP DRAW YOUR READER INTO THE STORY. INCLUDE A CHARACTER THAT READERS WILL LIKE AND ROOT FOR...LIKE ME...AND A CHARACTER THAT READERS WILL DISLIKE AND WANT TO BOO ON SIGHT...BARON VON BOREDOM, FOR EXAMPLE. IT'S ALSO A GOOD IDEA TO BRING FUNNY CHARACTERS INTO YOUR STORY FOR COMIC RELIEF.

WHY DON'T WE HAVE ANY FUNNY CHARACTERS, AVENGER?

OH, IF YOU ONLY KNEW, MY FUNNY LITTLE FRIEND. (PAUSE) THESE ARE JUST SOME IDEAS. TRY YOUR OWN COMBINATIONS OF CHARACTERS: MEN AND WOMEN, OLD PEOPLE AND BABIES, FLYING DOGS AND FLYING CATS.

RISING ACTION

INTRODUCTION

Horned Avenger Hint

Let brainstorms reign! Spend some time every day thinking up far-out settings, interesting characters, and especially crazy story ideas. Then write 'em down.

CLIMAX

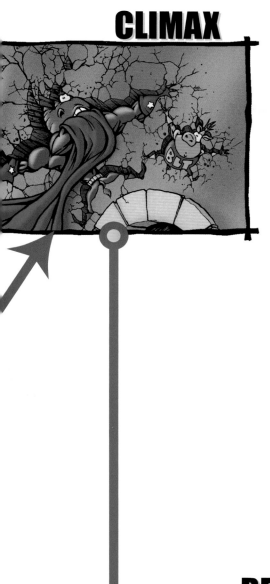

MIDDLE

THE *MIDDLE* OF A STORY IS WHERE PLOT AND CONFLICT BECOME IMPORTANT. YOU'VE GOT A GREAT SETTING THAT PROVIDES YOU WITH LOTS OF INTERESTING STORY POSSIBILITIES. YOU'VE GOT CHARACTERS WHO WILL INVOLVE READERS IN YOUR STORY. NOW, WHAT'S GOING TO HAPPEN IN YOUR STORY? YOU NEED A WAY TO STRUCTURE ALL THE GREAT STORY IDEAS YOU HAVE IN YOUR HEAD. THE *PLOT* IS THE EVENTS YOU DREAMED UP, LINKED TOGETHER TO TELL A STORY..

EVERY PLOT NEEDS A *PROBLEM* OR *CONFLICT*. THIS DOESN'T MEAN THERE HAS TO BE A WAR OR EVEN A PILLOW FIGHT. IT ONLY MEANS THAT SOMEONE IN THE STORY HAS TO WANT SOMETHING. IN OUR CASE WE WANT TO CAPTURE BARON VON BOREDOM SO HE WILL NOT BE ABLE TO END CREATIVITY.

THE *RISING ACTION* IS THE SERIES OF EVENTS THAT BUILD UP TO A CLIMAX. THE PROBLEM, OR CONFLICT, GETS MORE SERIOUS, OFTEN BECAUSE OF *COMPLICATIONS*. THE AUDIENCE IS KEPT IN SUSPENSE WHILE THEY WAIT TO SEE IF THE CONFLICT CAN BE RESOLVED. WE ARE AT THE CLIMAX PART OF OUR STORY RIGHT NOW. IF WE HAD BEEN FOLLOWING THE STRUCTURE OF THIS STORY, WE PROBABLY WOULD HAVE KNOWN SOMETHING LIKE THIS MOUNTAIN WAS GOING TO COME ALONG.

RESOLUTION

END

THE *END* OF THE STORY IS WHERE OUR CONFLICT IS SOLVED.

THE *CLIMAX* IS THE PLACE IN THE STORY WHERE EVERYTHING CHANGES. THE ORIGINAL PROBLEM IS SOLVED; THE CONFLICT ENDS.

EVEN AFTER THE MAIN PROBLEM IS SOLVED, THERE ARE PROBABLY STILL SOME LOOSE ENDS TO TIE UP. DURING THE *RESOLUTION*, YOU CAN CLEAR UP ALL THE COMPLICATIONS THAT YOU INTRODUCED DURING THE RISING ACTION. YOU CAN ALSO SHOW HOW THE CLIMAX AFFECTS VARIOUS CHARACTERS IN THE STORY.

WAIT A SECOND! SINCE WE DIDN'T SOLVE OUR ORIGINAL PROBLEM OR CONFLICT BY CATCHING VON BOREDOM, WHAT HAVE WE RESOLVED?!

WELL . . . WHEN A STORY DOESN'T HAVE A RESOLUTION, AND YOU HIT A WALL, OR CLIFF IN THIS CASE, YOU GET WHAT'S CALLED A CLIFF-HANGER. A CLIFF-HANGER IS—

HEY! WHAT ARE YOU GUYS DOIN' OUT OF YOUR CAGES?

OBVIOUSLY, YOU DON'T RECOGNIZE US. I AM THE HORNED AVENGER AND THIS IS MY PARTNER, BLT. WE ARE CRIME FIGHTERS CHASING THE EVIL BARON VON BOREDOM.

YOU HAVE TO GET UP PRETTY EARLY IN THE MORNING TO TRICK ME, MR. SMARTY SUPER HERO GUY. NOW YOU AND YOUR PORKY FRIEND HURRY UP AND GET BACK IN YOUR CAGES.

YEAH, YEAH, I'VE HEARD THAT A HUNDRED TIMES BEFORE.

AS I WAS SAYING, A CLIFF-HANGER IS WHEN THE ORIGINAL PROBLEM OR CONFLICT ISN'T RESOLVED, OR A NEW PROBLEM OR CONFLICT TAKES THE PLACE OF THE OLD ONE. . . .

UH-OH, H.A., I THINK WE ARE IN ONE OF THOSE CLIFF-HAMPERS. . . .

THOSE FOOLS! EVEN IF THEY ESCAPE, I HAVE A SURPRISE FOR THEM! HA! HA! HA! HA! HA! HA!

MUSE
GRAND O
DINOS
EXI

I SEE THE WORDS "TO BE CONTINUED . . ." OVER THERE!

TO BE CONTINUED . . .